THE SPOOKY B?X

MARK GONYEA

Henry Holt and Company • New York

Henry Holt and Company, LLC
Publishers since 1866
175 Fifth Avenue
New York, New York 10010
mackids.com

Henry Holt® is a registered trademark of
Henry Holt and Company, LLC.
Copyright © 2013 by Mark Gonyea
All rights reserved.

Library of Congress Cataloging-in-Publication Data
Gonyea, Mark.
The spooky box / Mark Gonyea. — 1st ed.
p. cm.
Summary: After viewing scary things that might slither, slice, or slide
their way out of a creepy black box, the reader is asked to lift the top
to reveal its contents.
ISBN 978-0-8050-8813-7 (hardcover)
1. Toy and movable books — Specimens. [1. Boxes — Fiction.
2. Toy and movable books.] I. Title.
PZ7.G5874Sp 2013 [E] — dc23 2012013528

First Edition — 2013
Printed in China by Macmillan Production Asia Ltd.,
Kwun Tong, Kowloon, Hong Kong [Vendor Code: 10]

1 3 5 7 9 10 8 6 4 2

FOR EVERYONE
WHO LOVES
THINKING
OF ENDLESS
POSSIBILITIES

KNOCK, KNOCK!

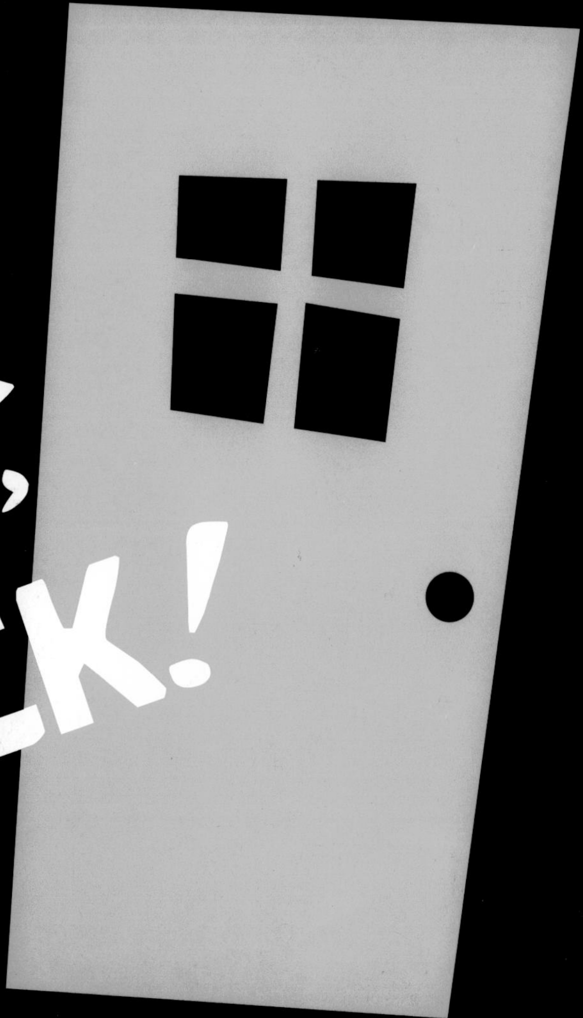

I wonder who that could be?

OH, IT'S A BOX!

A **SPOOKY** BOX.

I WONDER
WHAT'S **INSIDE?**

IT COULD
BE FULL OF
BATS!

OR FILLED
WITH
RATS!

MAYBE IT'S A **BUNCH** OF **OLD BONES!**

IT COULD BE
A **CAKE.**

OKAY, I'M GOING TO OPEN IT.

HERE I GO!

I KNOW.

YOU DO IT.
YOU OPEN IT!

IT MIGHT BE
FULL OF CANDY.

THUMP!

THUMP!

WHAT IS IT?

A **SQUID** FAR FROM HOME?

A TON OF
TOADS?

A CANDY-SEEKING ROBOT?

WITH LASER EYES AND A KUNG-FU CLAW!

THAT'S IT, I CAN'T TAKE IT.
LET'S OPEN IT!

ON THE COUNT OF THREE.
ONE ... **TWO** ...

TWO AND A HALF... THREE!

OPEN HERE

▼

TWO MORE
SPOOKY BOXES!

AHHHHGH!

THEY'RE PRETTY SMALL.
BUT **ANYTHING** COULD BE
INSIDE—LIKE A COUPLE OF
EVIL PUPPETS!

WHAT DO YOU THINK

COULD BE

INSIDE?